THIS BOOK IS DEDICATED TO ALL MY FRIENDS AND FAMILY
THAT HAVE SUPPORTED ME THROUGH THE YEARS.
THANKS FOR ENCOURAGING ME
TO FOLLOW MY DREAM!

HI! I'M AN APPLE SEED.

I'M A LITTLE COLD. I BETTER COVER UP.

THAT'S BETTER... BUT NOW I'M THIRSTY.

YAY! IT'S RAINING.

MMM...THIS WATER IS DELICIOUS!

THAT WAS SO GOOD! WATER HELPS ME GROW, TOO.

HMM... I FEEL DIFFERENT.

OH! I'M
GROWING!

I CAN FEEL THE SUNLIGHT. IT FEELS NICE!

I DID SO MUCH TODAY! BUT...

I THINK IT'S TIME FOR BED.

GOOD NIGHT!

GOOD MORNING!

I FEEL DIFFERENT TODAY.

WOW...
I GREW!

TODAY'S GOING TO BE AMAZING!

I WONDER IF I CAN GROW FASTER.

MAYBE IF I CLOSE MY EYES AND MAKE A WISH...

I DID IT! MY WISH CAME TRUE!

OH! WHAT ARE THOSE GREEN DOTS?

THEY'RE FLOWERS!

OH! THEY BLOOMED!

UH OH!
THE FLOWERS
ARE GONE.

HUH? THOSE GREEN THINGS ARE GROWING...

THEY KIND OF LOOK LIKE...

APPLES!

HI!